This
Treasure Cove Story
belongs to

TOY STORY

A CENTUM BOOK 978-1-913110-34-5
Published in Great Britain by Centum Books Ltd.
This edition published 2020.

1 3 5 7 9 10 8 6 4 2

Centum Books Ltd, 20 Devon Square, Newton Abbot,
Devon, TQ12 2HR, UK.

www.centumbooksltd.co.uk | books@centumbooksltd.co.uk
CENTUM BOOKS Limited Reg. No. 07641486.

A CIP catalogue record for this book is available
from the British Library.

Printed in China.

centum

Disney · PIXAR

Adapted by Kristen L Depken
Illustrated by Ben Butcher

Inspired by the art and character designs created by Pixar

Andy was a very lucky boy. He had lots of different **toys**. But his favourite toy was a cowboy named **Woody**.

Andy loved to
play with Woody.

But there was something Andy didn't know about Woody and the other toys. When Andy wasn't around, the toys had a life of their own. They **moved**. They **talked**. They **laughed**. And they had **adventures**.

All toys did. But only when no one was **watching**.

One year, Andy got a brand-new toy for his birthday — a space ranger named **Buzz Lightyear**! Buzz had flashing **lasers, gadgets** and even **wings**.

Soon Buzz became Andy's new favourite toy.
This made Woody very **sad**.

One day, Andy was going to Pizza Planet. His mum told him he could bring just one toy. Woody wanted to go! He tried to shove Buzz aside. But he accidentally pushed Buzz out of Andy's bedroom **window** instead. **Whoops!**

Woody got to go with Andy, but the other toys were very **upset**. They thought Woody had pushed Buzz out of the window on purpose.

Woody felt bad,
until Buzz turned
up in the car, too!

Buzz was **angry** with Woody. The two began to fight.
When the car stopped at a petrol station, they tumbled
out of the back door.

Oh, no! Andy and his mum drove off to Pizza Planet, leaving Buzz and Woody behind. They had become **lost toys!** And Andy's family was moving to a new home in just two days.

Then Woody spotted a
Pizza Planet truck. Woody
told Buzz the truck was
a spaceship and they
hopped on board.

Buzz insisted on sitting
in the front. Luckily,
a stack of pizza
boxes kept him
hidden from
the driver.

At Pizza Planet, Buzz climbed into a claw game filled with **toy aliens**. Buzz thought the game was a **spaceship**.

Woody tried to get Buzz out - but soon they were both trapped!

Oh, no! Andy's mean neighbour, **Sid**, captured Buzz and
Woody. Sid loved to torture toys. Woody and Buzz were
in **trouble**! Sid took Buzz and Woody home with him.

Sid's room was full of **mutant toys**. He had created them by combining different toy parts in strange ways... and now he had evil plans for Buzz and Woody! They had to escape.

Buzz tried to **fly** out of Sid's house, but he fell. He finally realised that Woody was right - he wasn't a real space ranger. He was only a **toy**.

Sid strapped a **rocket** to Buzz. He planned to blow Buzz to pieces! Buzz and Woody had to work **together** if they were going to escape.

But Buzz didn't want to escape. He felt sad because he wasn't a real space ranger. Woody helped Buzz understand that Andy loved him and that being a **toy** was very important.

And before they knew it, Buzz and Woody had become **friends**.

Woody came up with a plan to save Buzz. He asked **Sid's toys** to help. Just as Sid was about to **blow** Buzz up, Woody and the mutant toys came to life. Sid was **terrified** - he screamed and ran away!

Buzz and Woody were thrilled! So were Sid's toys. They knew that Sid would never torture them again.

Now Buzz and Woody were free to go back to Andy. But Andy's moving van was already pulling away from his house. They had to catch up with it!

Buzz and Woody ran and ran. Sid's mean dog, **Scud**, began to **chase** them!

Luckily, RC came out of the moving van to give Buzz and Woody a ride. They thought they were home free... until RC's batteries began to run out!

Then they remembered that Buzz still had Sid's
rocket strapped to his back. Woody launched it.
WHOOSH! Buzz, Woody and RC flew through the air.
RC landed safely in the back of the moving van. But
Buzz and Woody kept going.

Buzz popped open his **wings**. The rocket flew into
the air and exploded. Buzz and Woody were **falling**! But
thanks to Buzz's wings, they were falling with style. Buzz
held on to Woody and veered towards **Andy's car**.

Buzz and Woody glided through the car's **sunroof** and plopped down next to **Andy** - right where they belonged.

Treasure Cove Stories

Please contact Centum Books to receive the full list of titles in the *Treasure Cove Stories* series.
books@centumbooksltd.co.uk

Classic favourites

1 Three Little Pigs
2 Snow White and the Seven Dwarfs
3 The Fox and the Hound - Hide-and-Seek
4 Dumbo
5 Cinderella
6 Cinderella's Friends
7 Alice in Wonderland
8 Mad Hatter's Tea Party from Alice in Wonderland
9 Mickey Mouse and his Spaceship
10 Peter Pan
11 Pinocchio
12 Mickey and the Beanstalk
13 Sleeping Beauty and the Good Fairies
14 The Lucky Puppy
15 Chicken Little
16 The Incredibles
17 Coco
18 Winnie the Pooh and Tigger
19 The Sword in the Stone
20 Mary Poppins
21 The Jungle Book
22 The Aristocats
23 Lady and the Tramp
24 Bambi
25 Bambi - Friends of the Forest

Recently published

50 Frozen
51 Cinderella is my Babysitter
52 Beauty and the Beast - I am the Beast
53 Blaze and the Monster Machines - Mighty Monster Machines
54 Blaze and the Monster Machines - Dino Parade!
55 Teenage Mutant Ninja Turtles - Follow the Ninja!

56 I am a Princess
57 The Big Book of Paw Patrol
58 Paw Patrol - Adventures with Grandpa!
59 Paw Patrol - Pirate Pups!
60 Trolls
61 Trolls Holiday
62 The Secret Life of Pets
63 Zootropolis
64 Ariel is my Babysitter
65 Tiana is my Babysitter
66 Belle is my Babysitter
67 Paw Patrol - Itty-Bitty Kitty Rescue
68 Moana
69 Nella the Princess Knight - My Heart is Bright!
70 Guardians of the Galaxy
71 Captain America - High-Stakes Heist!
72 Ant-Man
73 The Mighty Avengers
74 The Mighty Avengers - Lights Out!
75 The Incredible Hulk
76 Shimmer & Shine - Wish Upon a Sleepover
77 Shimmer & Shine - Backyard Ballet
78 Paw Patrol - All-Star Pups!
79 Teenage Mutant Ninja Turtles - Really Spaced Out!
80 I am Ariel
81 Madagascar
82 Jasmine is my Babysitter
83 How to Train your Dragon
84 Shrek
85 Puss in Boots
86 Kung Fu Panda
87 Beauty and the Beast - I am Belle
88 The Lion Guard - The Imaginary Okapi
89 Thor - Thunder Strike!
90 Guardians of the Galaxy - Rocket to the Rescue!
91 Nella the Princess Knight - Nella and the Dragon
92 Shimmer & Shine - Treasure Twins!

93 Olaf's Frozen Adventure
94 Black Panther
95 Trolls - Branch's Bunker Birthday
96 Trolls - Poppy's Party
97 The Ugly Duckling
98 Cars - Look Out for Mater!
99 101 Dalmatians
100 The Sorcerer's Apprentice
101 Tangled
102 Avengers - The Threat of Thanos
103 Puppy Dog Pals - Don't Rain on my Pug-Rade
104 Jurassic Park
105 The Mighty Thor
106 Doctor Strange

Latest publications

107 Captain Marvel
108 The Invincible Iron Man
109 Black Panther - Warriors of Wakanda
110 The Big Freeze
111 Ratatouille
112 Aladdin
113 Aladdin - I am the Genie
114 Seven Dwarfs Find a House
115 Toy Story
116 Toy Story 4
117 Paw Patrol - Jurassic Bark!
118 Paw Patrol - Mighty Pup Power!
119 Shimmer & Shine - Pet Talent Show!
120 SpongeBob SquarePants - Krabby Patty Caper
121 The Lion King - I am Simba
122 Winnie the Pooh - The Honey Tree
123 Frozen II
124 Baby Shark and the Colours of the Ocean
125 Baby Shark and the Police Sharks!
126 Trolls World Tour

*Book list may be subject to change.